The Mistletoe Girl

and Other Christmas Stories

The Mistletoe Girl

and Other Christmas Stories

Ethel Pochocki

Illustrated by Peter LaGue

FOREST OF PEACE
Publishing
Suppliers for the Spiritual Pilgrim
Leavenworth, KS 66048

The Mistletoe Girl and Other Christmas Stories

copyright © 1999, by Ethel Pochocki

Library of Congress Cataloging-in-Publication Data

Pochocki, Ethel, 1925-
    The mistletoe girl, and other Christmas stories / Ethel Pochocki ; illustrated by Peter LaGue.
      p. cm.
    Contents: The mistletoe girl -- That's the way it was -- The white rabbit -- How M. Philippe spent Christmas -- Cat's Christmas -- The attic creche -- The baker's dog -- A Christmas tree for all seasons.
    ISBN 0-939516-47-0
     1. Christmas stories, American. I. Title: Mistletoe girl. II. Title.

PS3566.O25 M5 1999
813'.54--dc21

99-048856

published by
Forest of Peace Publishing, Inc.
PO Box 269
Leavenworth, KS 66048-0269 USA
1-800-659-3227
www.forestofpeace.com

printed in the U.S.A.

illustrations and cover design by
Peter LaGue

1st printing: October 1999
2nd printing: September 2001

Dedication

The Mistletoe Girl
is for
Elizabeth Goudge

Cat's Christmas
is for
Mamacat

with love

"You already have him," Balthazar said. "Your heart is his manger, and he is there now, warm as toast."

— *The Mistletoe Girl*

Ethel Pochocki is the author of many books of stories, including *A Penny for a Hundred*, *Rosebud and Red Flannel* and *The Wind Harp and Other Angel Tales*. She presently writes for *Cricket* and *Church World* magazines. Having raised eight children, she now lives with eight cats in the village of Brooks, Maine.

Peter LaGue is a freelance artist who lives on a farm in the beautiful prairie hills north of Wamego, Kansas. He spends his time writing music, drawing, sculpting, landscaping, gardening and studying how to live in union with the natural environment.

Table of Contents

Like clockwork, the gypsies arrived the week before the feast of St. Andrew, he who opened the door to the Christians' Advent. Each year they came to this village in Brittany, as they had done for generations beyond memory, to pick the mistletoe in the forest. From whence they came, no one knew or cared. Their coming and going was a temporary curiosity to the villagers, a seasonal happening, like the migrating of geese.

They did not like the gypsies; even more, they feared them. Their appearance was frightening, different. Their skin was dark and their flashing eyes fierce, and they were quick to smile and bow, as if they were planning no good. One never knew what went on in their minds. It was rumored they stole babies and goats and laundry right off the line. They dressed in long, dark, shabby clothes and wore too much jewelry and ate with their fingers. They talked in a strange language called Romany, instead of proper French, and, worst of all, they were pagans. It was sworn that if a gypsy walked into a church the statues would fall off their pedestals.

Yet the gypsies had to be tolerated, for they brought money to the village, money for the new clothes and toys and orange bonbons and roast duck for the Christmas feast. For the traveling people, as the villagers called them, were the only ones brave enough to venture into the winter forest to pick the mistletoe shrub, which would be packed and shipped to England. The English loved and paid well for the plant with its tradition of

bringing merriment to the holiday — and hung it from their doorways and stuck it in their buttonholes.

The gypsies didn't like the villagers either, and they kept to themselves by the edge of the forest where they camped in their gaily-painted wagons. Each day, whole families — except for the very old, who stayed back to watch the very young — left the camp in the dark before dawn with their knives and pruning hooks and long, pointed wicker baskets. They went deep into the woods where the mistletoe had fastened itself upon the tops of giant oaks and wild apple and poplars.

The mistletoe grew in such a fashion because, like the gypsies, it had no home of its own. But unlike the independent gypsies, the mistletoe had to live on its host tree for shelter and nourishment. An old gypsy legend said that once the mistletoe had been a proud, strong tree, but its wood had been used for the cross of Calvary, and for that it was condemned never again to touch the earth or have roots of its own. It was called a "tree thief" — an unfair judgment, the gypsies thought.

And so they filled the days inching towards Christmas cutting, scraping the shrub from the bark, the children throwing stones to knock down clumps or shinnying up the slender trunks, grabbing what they could. And at night they brought their brimming-full baskets, carried across their shoulders as oxen with their yokes, to the shippers. They eased their weariness by the campfires, eating their hedgehog or rabbit stew, content with what the day had given them.

Sara, the elder of the group, so wrinkled she looked like a dried apple doll, was also a healer and put soothing ointments on the gatherers' nicked and bleeding hands and gave them strong ginger tea to chase the cold from their bones.

Because of the gypsies' respect for Sara's age and wisdom, she lived in her own wagon with her granddaughter, Solange, whose parents had died, and the girl's pet hedgehog, Armand, whose parents had also died. This year Solange was finally old enough to join the other mistletoe girls — *manouches*, the shippers called them — in the woods. She was proud of her new privilege and worked as hard as any of them.

As she gathered, she wondered why the English made such a fuss over the little white berries. She knew they didn't use them as her grandmother did for healing or to wear as amulets around their necks to ward off evil. No, they used them to laugh and be foolish. Why?

She brought her question to Sara, who was wise and knew everything. And Sara told her the stories of the North People, of the enemies who kissed beneath the mistletoe and became friends, and how it thus came to mean joy at the Christmas feast.

"What *is* this Christmas?" asked Solange.

Sara made a pot of raspberry leaf tea, and as they sipped she told the story of the Holy Babe, the *Cretchuno*, whom the Christians called the Son of God, and of the Divine Mother, *De Deveieski*, and of her protector St. Joseph.

She spoke in low tones, rocking back and forth with her arms cradled as if she were the Madonna with the Babe.

"But if it is such a wonderful thing and they are so happy and sing songs and become friends," asked Solange, "why won't they share with us? Why do they say we are thieves and dirty and make things break if we go into their church?"

Sara laughed and shook her head. "Pay no attention, little one. They have always said that. What do they know? The Madonna knows our hearts, she knows our life — do you think she wore silks and satins in the stable? She knows we worship God and love the little *Cretchuno*. As for being thieves — I suppose it's how

you look at it. I remember a story my grandmother told me, that when the Lord Jesus was being nailed to the cross a gypsy boy ran off with a nail before the soldiers could use it. Of course the soldiers found another, but God did not forget his kindly act. So God allowed the gypsies to take what they wanted from the others and not count it as a sin."

Sara went on with more tales of the holy family while Solange, warm and content, blinked her eyes to keep awake. Did Solange know, Sara asked, that it was a gypsy woman who showed the Madonna how to spread the Holy Baby's laundry to dry on a rosemary bush to keep him smelling sweet? Did Solange know that one of the Magi, those learned men who traveled by the great star to pay respect to the Lord Jesus, was a gypsy chieftain? Yes, indeed, great Balthazar, who had come from Egypt, lived with his tribe here in France on the coast of Provence. Can you believe it, one of our own, at the stable!

Solange was no longer sleepy. Her eyes widened at this incredible news which Sara swore was fact. "So you see, child, we have even more right than others to be with them in church. If we choose to be."

Solange thought about this as the days grew short and near to Christmas. Each day her desire to see the Christians' creche, to hold the Babe, touch the Madonna,

grew stronger. She wanted to see the church; the place of mystery all lit by candles, as Sara said. She wanted to see the ceiling painted with angels and stars and clouds. She wanted to pay her respects, as her ancestor had done, with a bag of lavender and hops and sweet woodruff for under his pillow, and an amulet of mistletoe for his neck to ward off evil.

On the evening before Christmas, after the last berry had been picked and packed and shipped and was already making hearts merry in England, the gypsies began packing up the wagons. They put out the fires and fed the dogs and ponies one last good meal before they would set off in the morning. When the last baby had been sung to sleep, and the last spark turned to ash, and the stars burned bright in the cold sky, Solange quietly put on several layers of wool skirts and her thin black dancing boots. She pulled on a red shawl she had found in a trash bin in town before pulling a black velvet tam over her curly chocolaty hair. She put her gifts in her skirt pocket, and then, with Armand, set off for the church. It was snowing lightly.

She was frightened of the dark, as were most gypsies. Every tree that had been her daytime friend stood now dark and menacing, its black limbs reaching out like witches' bony fingers to grab her. She kept her eyes on the ground, swishing away the snow in quick, small steps. Armand followed in her path, whimpering a little. He would have preferred to stay in the wagon, but he was a loyal and true friend. Still, he wished Solange would remember he was not a dog.

Finally, after eluding tree roots and badger holes, Solange's heart and feet stopped racing. There in a clearing was the church, bursting with song and light within. The doors were already closed. Solange peered in through a low window steamed with the breath of hearty singers. She saw the priest swinging a gold bowl from which smoke was rising. The organ pumped and throbbed, and Solange could feel the music through the church walls.

Ah, it looked so warm and happy in there! She rubbed her stiffened fingers to warm them. Snow had gotten inside her boots, and she could feel nothing when she tried to wiggle her toes.

But when she saw the creche, she forgot every discomfort. How beautiful was the sweet family in their thatch-roofed stable! She could almost smell the fragrance of hay on the ground and the pine boughs framing the stable. There were shepherds and lambs and an ox and a cow and an angel — and surveying all, the

three Magi. Which one was Balthazar, she wondered, which one was hers?

In a little while, the singing and the preaching and the kneeling stopped, and the doors opened. People began emptying the church, rushing, hugging, kissing, dancing in the cold, eager to get home and to bed so the morning would come more quickly.

When everyone had gone, Solange, carrying Armand, slipped through the door and hid in the shadows behind a pillar. The priest, weary but happy in having had one more occasion to rejoice, snuffed out the candles, bowed to the holy family, and left.

Solange did not move, for once again the dark made her fearful. But she knew she had to see the Child and bring her gifts. She and Armand made their way with care down the aisle, helped by the faint moonlight coming through the windows, until they reached the altar and the creche at the foot of it. The moon shone suddenly stronger, and the silvery light made the scene look like a very old picture.

Solange knelt and carefully picked up the smiling carved Babe. She held him to her for a moment and then laid him back down. She tucked the bag of herbs under his pillow for sweet dreaming and tied the amulet around his neck. Then she turned to the Madonna and patted her

hands resting in her lap. "There now," she smiled, "you don't have to worry about him. Everything will be fine."

For a while, she just sat by the manger and looked into the Christ Child's eyes. He was so beautiful that she couldn't bear to leave him.

"I will take him with me," she thought. He was just a wooden doll. The church could get another. And did she not have a right to him?

Her toes and fingers were warm now, and she lay her head down on the manger, feeling sleepy with the warmth and smell of pine. She would rest a while before the dreaded trip home in the dark.

But her eyes could not stay closed, for the silvery light was turning brighter and golden. It was so bright it forced her eyes to open completely. She heard a silky rustling and a clittery clanking. She turned slowly, afraid to look, only to find a very tall, strong, dark-skinned man with a curly beard looking down at her, smiling. He stood there in full golden shimmering pants and a green tunic embroidered in jewels. Large golden hoops hung from his ears and up his arms, and his thick curly black hair was wrapped in a turban of many-colored silks. In the center of the headdress was a sapphire in the shape of a comet.

Solange lost all fear. "Balthazar!" she cried. She

bowed deeply before the Magi, her kinsman.

"Dear Solange!" he spoke in a booming voice that echoed through the pews. Armand hid under the manger.

"I came to bring him gifts," said Solange, not knowing what else to say.

"I, too," said Balthazar. "Are we not fortunate to be alone with him? Tomorrow there will be so many people. But that is how it should be. He comes for all of us." Balthazar looked into Solange's eyes, and she knew he knew what she had been planning.

Solange looked away. "I would have brought him back," she said.

"Would you?" asked Balthazar.

"I would never steal a *real* baby," Solange said, not answering his question. "This was only a doll. I wanted him for myself."

"But you already have him. He is already yours, the real Child. If you want him. Your heart is his manger, and he is there now, warm as toast."

Solange did not understand this. But before she could ask more questions, Balthazar clapped his hands and boomed, "Now, enough talk, the Babe is here and we are here and it is a time to be joyful!" He pulled a tambourine from his ballooning

pants and beat upon it. He began to sing, a gentle song that Solange knew, and then dance, a weaving, back-and-forth circling dance. Solange jumped up and joined him. They danced in front of the creche, Armand trying clumsily to keep up with them. Then, twirling still in circles, they whirled up the aisle. The sweet laughter of the little girl and the deep, mellow singing of the Magi settled into the walls and wood of the church.

When they were nearly exhausted, Balthazar said, "We must leave now."

"*We?*" asked Solange.

"You don't think I would let a kinsman travel the dark alone, do you? And on our way I will tell you more about the Lord Jesus and the comet star that guided us to him."

They went out into the snowy night to where his camel waited. The Magi helped Armand into a saddlebag, and then he and Solange climbed astride the camel. "I usually ride an Arabian," he explained, but my companions travel by camel and offered me one. It would have been ungracious to refuse."

High above the ground, Solange felt as if she were mistress of the universe. Snowflakes melted and glistened on her hair like stars. Before they knew it, they were at the door of Sara's wagon.

Balthazar deposited Solange and Armand on the

ground. "Now, little one," he said, "I have a gift for you. No," he smiled, "not the jewel in my turban you eye so longingly."

Solange blushed, for she had not thought he had seen her quick, yearning look.

"If I gave it to you, even your own would say you stole it and take it from you, and you would have nothing. I give you something better, something only you would want."

From his saddlebag he brought a small green shrub, bristly as Armand, in a blue china pot that was the color of the Madonna's robe.

"May your life be as sweet and fresh and full of green hope as this rosemary plant. Take it with you in your wagon, and when you decide to travel no more plant it wherever you live. It will grow into a tree, giving shelter to thrush and squirrel and other travelers. And every time you look at it you will remember this night and our dance of joy. Is this not better than a jewel?"

Solange thought she really would have liked the sapphire, for she loved bright, sparkly things. But she also cherished what she held in her hand, something of her own to love and care for. She brushed its needles gently against her cheek. As with Armand's, if you brushed them just so, they wouldn't prick you.

When she looked up to thank the Magi, he was not there. He was gone, soundlessly, as if he had never been, as if they had not danced and rode together on a camel through the woods.

Solange told Sara everything, and Sara believed her because there was always truth between them. She put the rosemary in the window by her cot. The needles gave off a sharp freshness, covering the smell of old frying grease. Solange fell asleep and dreamed of the Madonna washing the Child's clothes and spreading them to dry on Solange's rosemary bush, which had already grown into a fat, round tree.

On Christmas morning, old Henri, the church's caretaker, opened the doors and began to brush away the snow that had fallen during the night. He stopped to look at some strange tracks in the snow, tracks he had never seen before.

They could not belong to any animals in the village. They almost looked like…camel tracks. He knew this was not possible, since there were no camels in Brittany. He finished sweeping, shook the snow from his hair and the broom, and stood in the back of the church, joining in the joyous carols.

On the heart of the woods, there lived an oak tree that was greatly respected for its age and wisdom by all the other trees and animals and birds who lived there. It was glorious to look upon, especially when it turned golden brown in the autumn. All the acorns that went to sleep in the ground beneath it dreamed that they would grow up to be as grand. Yet with all its gifts, the oak tree was not vain or haughty. It graciously welcomed all visitors, whether they were hawks or hummingbirds or humans.

One day the tree felt something on a topmost branch, something like an itch and a twitch and a grabbing, something that refused to be shaken off by the wind. The oak was curious. It was used to birds building nests and small animals racing up its trunk, but these creatures stayed only a short time and then left. This stranger seemed to be making itself at home. It grew bigger and began to spread, leaving clumps of green here and there on other branches.

The oak decided to speak to its guest. "I beg your pardon," it said. "I don't know your name, but I was wondering just how long you plan to stay. It's not that you're a bother, but it does feel strange not knowing what's going on up there." The tree did not want to sound inhospitable, but it felt it had a right to know.

The shrub replied in a friendly, eager-to-please manner. "The name's Mistletoe. A bird dropped me off. I said to him, 'Drop me off on that strong, handsome oak' — you do stand out, you know — so here I am. I'm afraid you're stuck with me."

The oak tree was flattered but still puzzled. "Thank you very much, but I don't understand — I'm stuck with you?"

"Forever. Till death do us part. There's nothing I can do about it. That's the way it is. It's the family curse," sighed the plant.

The oak's sympathetic heart went out to the mistletoe.

"Now, now," it comforted, "that's all right. I don't mind the company. And what's this about a family curse? You look attractive and healthy to me."

"Well," began the mistletoe, "the story is that years and years ago we were trees as tall and spectacular as you oaks are. One day some soldiers came and chopped down one of us and used the wood for the cross on Calvary. Because of this, God said our roots could never again touch the earth. We could never live on our own. We would have to depend on the kindness of strangers."

"Oh, I can't believe that," said the shocked oak. "That doesn't seem fair at all. I don't think God would do that. God doesn't hold a grudge. Besides, it wasn't your fault. The humans did the deed."

"You're right, we had nothing to say about it. But facts are facts. We have no roots. That's the way it is."

"But what do you live on — air?" asked the oak.

"I live on you," the mistletoe said quietly. "I'm sorry, but that's the way it is."

"*That* doesn't seem fair either," said the surprised oak, whose nourishment came from its roots deep within the earth. The tree was beginning to get a little upset now. But it saw the mistletoe's embarrassment in admitting that it was a beggar — some would say a thief — and said, "Well, now, I suppose we could share the food. You are very small, after all, and I have enough strength to feed us both, seeing as that's how it is."

And so the mistletoe and the oak lived together for many years. The mistletoe spread and covered all the topmost branches, and the oak's generosity began to sap its own strength. It no longer put forth spring leaves, and its bark turned brittle and gray and began to peel. In wintry ice storms or summer gales its now-feeble branches broke and fell. The old tree looked like a gnarled old woman with green curly hair and clumps of pearls bedecking it.

One day, Christmas Eve day to be exact, a poor young man came to the woods with his ax and sled. He walked as though he carried the burdens of the world, stopping every now and then to pull up his drooping socks and sigh deeply. He wished for something wonderful to happen. He was out of money and could buy no food or firewood, for he could find no work. Even worse, he was newly married and could give his darling wife no present for Christmas. That didn't matter, she told him cheerfully, for she had nothing to give him either.

"But we shall have a tree! I can at least do that!" he vowed. His wife bundled him up in his mittens and

drooping kneesocks and the ten-foot-long stocking cap she'd knitted him, and off he went to the woods.

In no time at all he found a short, plump, motherly little fir that would fit perfectly in their cottage. They had no decorations, but he knew that his wife, the cleverest woman who ever lived, would make the tree into a thing of beauty.

He looked up at a pair of scolding chickadees and gasped. The topmost branches of a dead oak tree hung heavy with clumps of evergreen and white berries. Mistletoe! He shinnied up the tree, cut off all the plants he could reach, and let them drop into the snow.

When he had gathered as much mistletoe as the sled could carry, he went into town and sold every single bit, except for one sprig. Then he bought eggs and crusty dark bread and a wheel of Swiss cheese and a ham with slices of pineapple on it and a dozen cinnamon buns with frosting, and he still had money left over.

His heart feathery light, he returned to the woods to pick up his ax and the firtree, which he'd left behind. He looked once more at the oak, now even more forlorn without its decorations. What a bounty of firewood it would give, he thought. What better than a toasty hearth to make the holiday complete?

He was sorry that the tree was dead, but that's the way it was. He began to chop away at the limbs and split them into small logs. When he had enough wood for that evening and Christmas Day, he loaded it onto his sled, along with the firtree and Christmas goodies he had bought in town. He would return for the rest of the oak tree after Christmas and bring it home a sled at a time.

What joy there was in the cottage when the husband arrived home and showed his wife what his trip to the woods had brought about! He nailed the sprig of mistletoe over the doorway and caught his wife under it and kissed her, laughing, "Now, my turtledove, here is the best gift of all!"

"And now, *my* turtledove," she laughed, kissing him back, "I return it, so we're even. You cannot love me more than I love you!"

The husband set about making a fire, and soon a rosy warmth spread through the cottage and into their eyes and cheeks and hearts.

The wife sliced the crusty bread and meat and cheese and got out the mustard and set the table, humming all the while.

After they ate their dinner, they decorated the tree with bits of colored yarn and lace and hair ribbons. Then they sat by the fire, licking frosting from their fingers, and blessed the oak and the mistletoe for giving them warmth and food and joy. And that's the way it was.

There was once a small brown rabbit who never had time to bask in the midday sun or dance in the moonlight or eat a leisurely dinner with friends. She lived a frantic life of endless motion, racing, dodging, hiding from her enemies in crevices or thickets. It was not a happy way of life, but she knew no other, for, as it is with all the small animals of the forest, her stronger enemies were always ready to pounce and end that life.

The little rabbit often sat frozen; not daring to twitch or breathe when the shadow of the plummeting eagle darkened the grass or the horrid screech of the snow owl slashed across the night air. Her brothers and sisters had been snatched by a hawk searching for dinner morsels, and since then she had gone her solitary way along the rabbit highways of the meadow.

Sometimes there was something in her that longed to do the unexpected, to be carefree, to leap across frozen streams in daylight, to dance in the light of the full moon, even though to do so, she knew, was to court trouble.

On one such day in October, she felt the urge to frolic with the wind, who tossed a rain of scarlet maple leaves upon her in glee. So caught up with laughter was she that she did not hear the soft step of the fox upon the dried leaves. She was rolling on the ground, her eyes closed, the wind rippling her fur, when she looked up to find the long, pointed snout of the fox above her. She lunged and leaped, her heart beating madly, and bounded

into the woods. The fox followed close behind her, in no great hurry, since he was certain she would be his dinner, when a porcupine sat directly in his path, squat and hostile, causing the fox to stop and survey the situation. The rabbit, on the other hand, did not look back but tore madly farther into the woods.

She came upon a great commotion of birds, and her heart rose up with hope. There amidst the assembly of chickadees, bobolinks, wrens, linnets and robins stood a little man in a coarse gray robe. He seemed to be directing them in a hymn. She fell in exhaustion at his feet, certain that Brother Francis would not harm her.

When her breath returned, she told him of her weariness of running, always running from her enemies. The birds stopped singing and listened with sympathy. "Soon it will be winter and the snows will come," she sighed, "and it will be worse. I shall have not even the grass to hide in. I shall stick out like a sore thumb — or a brown rabbit. I don't sleep away the winter as the bears do. I must go out and look for dead grasses or birch bark or wild canes of raspberry. And wherever I go, the fox and weasel wait to pounce. I know they are your brothers, but they surely aren't mine."

Brother Francis soothed the quivering animal in his arms. "Yes, I know it takes some of us longer than others to learn we are all children of one Father. We are all brothers and sisters. I cannot change the heart or nature of Brother Fox. He, in turn, is also hunted by dogs and wolves and men.

"You already have the gift of fleetness, the swiftness that all envy. Now I will ask God to give you the gift of a snowsuit. Soon your brown fur shall turn white, a little at a time in the next few weeks, so that by the time of the first snowfall, you shall blend into the snow as if you did not exist. Only the tips of your ears and your nose will stay black."

The rabbit leaped into the air and turned a somersault and, when she landed, drummed the ground with her hind legs to show her joy. Her friend, Brother Wind, answered with a song through the tops of the aspens, and the sound was like the tinkling of a hundred fairy tambourines.

And so, day by day, the fur of the brown rabbit grew whiter, and thick soles of hair grew on her feet so she might glide lightly over the crust of snow as if on showshoes. By December, she had become an invisible ghost-rabbit who foraged the hills and nibbled the hips of thorny rosebushes unseen. She was still cautious, burrowing into the snow

when the eagle swooped low or when she heard, with her marvelous ears, a soft step in the brush.

But when the full moon shone upon her in its silvery brilliance, something happened to the timid rabbit. She became fearless and threw caution to the wind, who caught it and held it until she was through dancing. She danced on the hillside, sometimes with other rabbits, sometimes by herself, and often with her shadow.

The rabbit seemed bewitched by the moon's beauty, staring up with long, loving longing, as if wondering what lay beyond the silver orb's cool indifference. Suddenly, she would be unable to contain herself any longer. She would dart off, churning up pinwheels of snow, which would cling to her whiskers and nose and ears as she danced her circle dance, weaving in and out of trees and rocks and coming back to where she had started.

It was on such a moonlit night, with the snow falling and mounding into peaks swirled high like meringue, that the rabbit seemed more moon-touched than ever. She scampered ledges and ravines as if in a great hurry to get somewhere, although where she had not the faintest idea.

There was something in the air — an expectancy — that froze her breath. Her ears heard the faint pealing of bells in a town past the hills. The music of the chimes bounced off the snowy hilltops back into the valley where the rabbit sat thinking her long thoughts.

A stream of light from an unblinking star joined the moonlight. The rabbit's hind legs began to drum in the excitement of the unknown. She washed her face, wetting her paw and rubbing it over her nose and whiskers and ears. Something was going to happen — she could feel it!

Very soon, it did. Brother Francis, followed by a raggle-taggle band of creatures from the wood, came into the clearing, walking and singing in the most raucous manner. The white rabbit sat still, unbreathing, and lowered her ears, which hurt from the noise. The magpie cawed and black sheep bleated, owls screeched, foxes barked, the cock crowed and a chipmunk scolded them all.

On his arms Brother Francis carried a wooden manger, in which lay a doll made of socks and scraps, with a large smile painted on its face. It belonged to a poor child in the village. The doll lay on a pile of hay and dried wildflowers cut down in their prime in the summer reaping. The

rabbit's nose twitched at the sweet smell and her stomach tightened with hunger.

Brother Francis found a space beneath a golden larch and brushed away the snow. He placed the manger under a protecting low branch, knelt and clasped his hands before it. The star beamed its light upon the little man and the doll in the manger and the still-singing animals.

The white rabbit could not believe what she was seeing — the fox and the cat and the owl and the sheep and the dog who guarded the sheep, all gathered about the manger, singing with great joy and very little harmony:

> Sing unto the Lord
> *bark-bark* and *squeak*
> A new song tonight!
> *whinny* and *bleat*
> Sing out his praise
> *crackle* and *screech*
> From the ends of the earth!
> *whistle* and *coo*
> And a little Child
> *bray* and *mew*
> Shall lead us all
> blackbird and blue
> To our Father in heaven!
> *cock-a-doodle-do*!

Above the manger hovered the turtledove and thrush and linnet, who sang so sweetly the others ceased their racket. The beauty of the birds' song had pierced the other creature's hearts; they could not speak.

The rabbit watched all this from the hill where she had danced in the moonlight. She wanted to join in their singing if only by thumping, but she did not trust her enemies, no matter how joyously they were singing. She hung back, fitting into the snow as a piece in a jigsaw puzzle.

As she sat up, her paws folded before her, the moon cast her shadow. It fell as a giant presence over all the animals — the songbirds weaving in and out of the shadow-ears — so her nearness was felt by each of them.

"Sister Rabbit," Brother Francis called to her softly, "come and join us. This is the night of the Christ Child's birth, and we need every voice to give him praise. See, he longs to share his love with all his children."

"I am afraid," she whispered back. "I do not trust enough to love. I fear to see my blood upon the snow if I stand too close to Brother Fox."

"Come," he said again, "leap into my arms and lay your fluttering heart against mine, and you will be safe."

Her shadow withdrew from the group and darted about the larch trees, until she bounded high into the midnight sky and fell into his waiting arms. He comforted the shivering rabbit, who was not sure she had done the right thing. All her enemies were here, surrounding her, yet none rose to claim her life.

Instead, they all gazed upon the manger, which now was bathed in a warm golden light coming from within. The doll of scraps and socks was no longer there. In its place lay a real child of smiles who reached up his hand to bless Brother Francis and his friends.

The white rabbit wriggled free of Francis' arms and hopped into the manger. She wanted to pay her small homage to the Christ Child too. She began pulling the white fur from her breast until she had enough to make a coverlet for the Child. The other animals watched and murmured approval over the gift. "Not even my wool is as soft," said the black sheep. The Child touched the rabbit's black nose and laughed. And so it was on that special night that they sat and talked and agreed and shared wisps of the fragrant hay.

"Tonight," said Brother Francis, "we are at peace with one another. We put aside our hungers and ravaging. We sheathe our talons and fangs and cunning hearts and become brothers and sisters in the Christ Child's love. Wind and rain, fox and fire, catkin and woolly bear — we are all children of the one Father. Let us rejoice, for tonight we have a new Brother!"

Soon the dark sky was streaked with rose. The sun took charge, and the moon rolled over and went to sleep. The farm animals followed Brother Francis as he carried the manger back to the village. The mice and the moles had left in the dark for their underground homes, and the owl already sat sleeping in his tree perch. The fox and the weasel hurried into the woods, quietly, businesslike.

The white rabbit once again became a ghost, an unseen dervish running in circles, leaving only a dizzying maze of tracks, a moonshadow and a blanket of fur for a child's doll to prove she really did exist.

How
M.Philippe
Spent
Christmas Eve

Once, a long, long time ago in the Old Forest, something strange happened on Christmas Eve. Happily strange it was, but puzzling, nonetheless. It has grown into a legend among the animals, and to this day they tell it to the little ones on the holy night.

It has to do with one of their own, M. Philippe, a fox of high esteem and a pillar of the community. He exemplified the best of the fox-character — a brilliant, cunning wit, exquisite manners, charming humor and, in all his movements, a delicate gliding grace. It was a joy to watch him fence or dance a minuet. He also had a touch of the poet in his soul, an eye for truth and beauty in all he encountered. He revered all life, even the animals he felt bound to kill.

He did not understand why this was so, only that it was. "Life is a mystery," he would sigh as he looked to the night sky and the world beyond the stars.

M. Philippe was also a cook of great artistry. When he gave a party, everybody came. He knew where to find the herbs and blossoms for wine, the wild leeks and mushrooms for his rabbit stew and chicken and dumplings, the tiny crabapples for fritters and caraway seeds for cookies. When the moon rose, he picked the young peas and beans and onions, while the cats and dogs and humans slept.

And then, swift and deadly as an arrow, he would catch the chickens and rabbits for his famous feasts. He told himself that this was just part of being a fox. It was the way he

must follow — he had no choice.

Robins eat worms, cats eat robins, foxes eat chickens and rabbits. It was the way. And so he kept on stalking and catching and killing and cooking.

But as the years passed, M. Philippe yearned less and less to stalk his prey, knowing that one quick movement would end their lives. He would much rather enjoy the antics of the foolish chickens and scatterbrained rabbits from the tall grass. "If only I could change the way," he would sigh before he bagged his meal for the evening.

And so it was, this night before Christmas, that M. Philippe set out in air as crisp and brittle as an icicle. He picked some wild grapes hanging from vines he could reach and cranberries from the bog. They were a bit shriveled from the frost but would be delicious in a sauce for his Lemon-Garlic Chicken.

He sang softly to himself, and the steam from his breath rose like wispy grace notes:

A fox went out a chilly night,
He prayed the moon for it to give him light...

He needed no moon for light, he thought, for every star in the universe was like a jewel on display in the black velvet sky, burning silver bright, twinkling, winking; some even seemed to turn to gold if one stared at them long enough. M. Philippe, in his white gloves and red plaid scarf, his basket of woven willow strips over his arm, stood motionless on the small hill at the edge of the forest and looked up at the stars for a long while.

He thought of all the years the stars had looked down upon the forests and foxes before him — what stories they could tell! Did they shine as bright on the first Christmas as they did this night?

What must it have been like? He'd heard from a storyteller who had passed through the Old Forest that on this special night all the animals were friends, that they could talk and sing and give praise as the humans did. He would have liked that: one night when he would not have to kill or cause pain or skulk off like a murderer. Of course, he quickly reassured himself he was not a murderer.

He was simply acting according to his nature. Wasn't he?

One star seemed to grow stronger as he watched it, almost blinding him. He felt compelled to stare deeply into it, into the fiery center of the golden orb, where he saw a picture. A small Child lay in a manger, bathed in golden rays coming from a hole in the heavens. Around

the crude bed knelt the animals of the farm and woods and jungle. A huge, proud lion stood at the head of the manger above the Child, as if he were the figurehead on a boat. Wolves, lambs, squirrels, mourning doves, a goose, an owl, rabbits, all smiled at him and each other. A black-and-white cat purred at his feet, and a dozen baby chicks spilled out from his hands.

M. Philippe stood transfixed, smiling back, and then a great sadness came upon him. He saw no fox at the manger. "Why," he asked the Child, "cannot a fox feel and love and adore as well as a wolf? Why," he asked again, feeling tears rise, "am I not there?"

The Child heard and reached through the dark eons of space and stroked the fox's ear. "Love me," he whispered, "as I love you. Love one another as I love you. We are all brothers and sisters."

The fox did not understand, but the warmth of the Child's touch spread to his heart and made it so light that he felt as if 100 balloons were inside his body. He wanted to leap and dance and sing. Could it be that simple? Just *love*? The Child and the animals went back into the star, and from behind it the fox heard laughter and singing as sweet and light as the wind teasing glass wind chimes. He longed to be part of that joy!

"You can," sang his heart. "Change your way! Take a different path! Be his brother!" As he stood there, not knowing how to do this, he saw the large white ball moving toward him, crazily charging like a snowplow across the open field. The moon cast the shadow of large haunches, feet and flattened ears, a body leaping high into the air.

Suddenly, Achille, the largest snow shoe hare in the forest, stopped and froze. His heart almost stopped beating, for many of his relatives had contributed to M. Philippe's culinary reputation. He saw the fox move lightly, precisely, down the path toward him. So this is how it would end, thought Achille, not daring to move even his eyes. His loved ones would wait in vain for him to come home. Alas, he would be the fox's Christmas dinner instead. There was no way he could escape the fox, who was now so close the hare could feel his breath.

The fox bowed to Achille. "Good evening, my friend Achille. Is it not a lovely, starry night? I wish you and yours a happy celebration. *Bon soir*!" He bowed again and continued on his way, his scarf blowing behind him in the rising wind.

He stopped by a jack-o-lantern inhabited by a mouse family. Its features had softened from a fierce Halloween scowl to a sunken quizzical look, not unpleasant. Through the windows, which had been the pumpkin's eyes, he saw the mouse children trimming their tiny tree and the father and mother roasting acorns over the cedar-shavings fire. He felt another pang. Oh to be part of a family, warm and snug inside their little world! A tender feeling for them — was it love? — spread through him. He wanted to protect them and keep their lives forever contented. Dear little creatures — he could imagine them scampering over the hay of the manger, too quick for even the Child to catch them!

He went on, for he was in a hurry to reach the henhouse before midnight. He had made a good beginning. He had bowed to Achille and made pleasantries with him; he had loved the mice from afar. Now, giddy with newfound joy, he would dare to act in the most unfox-like manner. He would visit the chickens, wish them *joyeux noel* and leave with his basket empty.

He sang again and danced in tune:

Fox ran till he came to the farmer's bin,
Where the ducks and geese were kept therein,
following the well-worn path to the henhouse.

Laughter and whispers and singing came from within, and above it all, the loud, shrill clucking of buxom Madame Sylvie, the mother of the little brood of chicks (six daughters, one son).

The door, hung with a wreath of balsam and strawflowers, was slightly ajar, and M. Philippe, not quite sure of what he should do, stood listening.

"Come, come, children," sang Madame Sylvie shrilly, "it's getting late, and your mother is tired even if you aren't. Gather round — Estelle, you're spilling your popcorn, take care! — and I'll tell you the story of the first Christmas and the rooster who was the first to spread the good news to the shepherds. The humans think the angels did it, but we know better!"

The shadow of M. Philippe, who had gently pushed the door open upon the loving scene, fell across the room and covered the baby chicks like a dark blanket. Madame Sylvie turned quickly and gave a small shriek. No, not tonight, not on this sacred night! How could the Child allow the dreaded enemy to strike tonight? She had lost many of her brothers and sisters to him — now would he take her little ones also?

Anger wiped out fear, and in her outrage she spoke boldly to the fox, "M. Philippe," for, of course, she knew who he was, "how dare you spoil this holy eve? Have

you no manners, no respect for the Child? Do you not have a heart as well as a stomach? How can you kill on Christmas Eve?"

The little chicks cheeped and ran under her skirt for safety.

"Madame Sylvie," answered the fox," I come only to wish you well this night, and to bring you this small gift. Consider me, if you will, a solitary Wise Man." He emptied his basket of wild grapes and cranberries at her feet.

Madame Sylvie looked deep into the fox's eyes and said nothing. She was a wise creature who knew that life is a mystery. This could be a clever ruse. Then again, it might not. If it were, they would all die. If it were not, then life was even more mysterious than she had imagined. In either case, she would not be guilty of bad manners.

"It is most kind of you to remember us, sir. Children, say *thank you* to M. Philippe." The chicks came out from under her skirt, cheeping in delight over such unexpected delicacies that came from beyond their world of fenced-in yard. "And you, monsieur, will you accept some small gifts from us in return?"

She went into her kitchen and brought out a bag of dried mushrooms, a pot of chives, a small round of goat's cheese, six brown eggs and a small jar of yellow syrup. "For your Christmas dinner, and the ginger syrup is my mother's recipe, good for colds and stomach upset."

They bowed to each other and said good-night, and the fox, carrying his precious gifts with care, danced his way home by the light of the star.

On the cold and frosty Christmas Day, he made a cheese soufflé so elegant, so delicious, the likes of it has not been tasted before or since. It was a miracle soufflé that seemed to have no end, for it fed all who came to the feast. We do not know if this happened every Christmas Day thereafter, or if M. Philippe was moved by Love just this once. All we know is that it happened, and that life is a mystery.

Cat's Christmas

From the barn cupola, Cat watched intently as an old woman moved into the large, white house connected to the barn. It was a handsome old house, with a wraparound porch and windows bordered in colored glass and a turret on the third floor that looked like a witch's hat. The old woman thought it would be the perfect home for her and her family of cats. There were five of them, all related, all marvelously marbled in patterns of black and white.

Most of the time everyone got on well together, but there were times when the cats tried the old woman's patience. Sometimes they would pounce on her lap when she read the paper or tangle her yarn when she was knitting. Or they would lick the butter and steal sausages right off her plate. And when she went to bed, they would curl up so close to her she couldn't turn over, and they would nibble on her nose to wake her in the morning.

Then she would explode, "Drat you, cats! I shall give you all away if you don't behave!" The cats would just smile and lick their paws, because they knew better.

Cat waited a few days to let the family settle in, and then she made her move. One morning the old woman opened the door to get her paper and found Cat sitting on the porch. She glared at the animal. Cat, smiling broadly and confidently, ignored the look.

She was not a beautiful or even an attractive cat. She was old and mangy, with scrawny toothpick legs and a long, ratty tail that looked as if it had been slammed in a door. Her black and white fur, matted with thistle burrs, was not arranged in a pattern

pleasing to the eye. It was as if a bottle of black ink had spilled over her white face, ran down over her nose and settled into a mustache beneath it. Never in my life, thought the old woman, have I seen such an ugly cat.

Cat, however, had no such image of herself. "Good morning, madam," she smiled. "Welcome to your new home. *Our* new home, I should say, since I have been with the manor since I was an infant, even though I have temporarily taken quarters in the barn. It has been such a refreshing change, rollicking in the hay, enjoying the music of the crickets, so pleasant! But it will be good to return to the kitchen hearth once again, now that autumn is nigh." Her whiskers quivered in anticipation.

The woman was alarmed. "Oh, dear no, I'm sorry," she said, "but I already have five cats on my hearth and I don't need even one more. I'm afraid you'll have to find another home." The old woman started to close her front door, but Cat adroitly whipped out her leg and held the door ajar.

"Madam, you don't understand. I come with the house. I am part of the package. I live here and am willing to share it with you and," she shuddered slightly, "your animals."

"Sorry, Cat," the old woman said briskly, "but I do not want any more cats. Five are quite enough."

"You may stay in the barn, if you like," added the old woman, feeling a bit guilty.

"Madam, I am already in the barn," Cat answered, huffily. "I don't need your permission to do so." And she waddled off in a snit.

That evening the old woman brought a saucer of milk and a bowl of dry cat food out to the barn but didn't stay to socialize. Cat could hear her cooing to the cats inside the house, "Here, Minnie, pretty Minnie…. Pansy, you little puffball, come and eat…."

Disgusting, absolutely disgusting, thought Cat, as she sat atop a pile of squashes and picked sawdust out from between her toes. It wasn't right that those lazy creatures should sit in the window, licking sardine oil off their paws, while she sat pining away in the barn.

She tried to squeeze a tear out at the unfairness of it all. Not succeeding, she stretched out her sagging body and yawned. Never mind, she told herself; it won't be this way for long. "If all goes well, by this time tomorrow, the old woman will find me irresistible, and I shall be curled up, toasty and warm, under her kitchen stove."

Then Cat hopped into a large red flowerpot and went to sleep.

Early the next morning, the old woman was startled awake by an urgent knocking at the front door. She rushed down the stairs and opened the door cautiously. There stood Cat, with a grin from ear to ear. She wore a red sweater with a white letter **C** on the front, a green plaid skirt, white socks, which had fallen down her skinny legs, and black-and-white saddle shoes. Two very short ponytails tied with red yarn stuck out from under her ears. A bookbag stuffed with lumpy objects was slung over one shoulder.

The old woman could hardly keep from laughing but managed to ask politely, "Yes, can I help you?"

"Good morning, madam," beamed Cat. "I hope I didn't wake you?"

"Umph," grunted the old woman, wrapping her robe tightly around her shivering bones.

"Good. My name is Mary Lu Citronella, and I live down the road. I am working my way through college selling my handmade potholders and horse chestnut wind chimes. I heard that you just moved in and I wondered if…."

"That's very interesting. What college?"

"The Sarah B. Catnip College of Felinary Arts."

"I see. I've heard of it. I thought it closed down last year."

Cat never twitched a whisker. "I'm afraid, Madam, that you must be mistaken. I just this week finished my courses in *History of the Churchmouse* and *Creative Whisker Trimming*. Now, if I might step inside to show you my work…."

"Sorry, Miss Citronella. Wind chimes drive me crazy, and I already have too many potholders — and cats. Besides, aren't you a little old to be going to school?"

Cat snapped her bag shut, tossed her head and walked off, muttering, "One is never too old to learn

something new and to open one's mind...."

"Yes, indeed," the old woman called after, and then shut the door smartly.

The next morning, as she was washing the breakfast dishes, the old woman heard a thud and then a feeble moaning on the back porch. She opened the door and there lay Cat, prone upon the doorstep, in a pink flannel nightgown.

"Good heavens," cried the old woman. "What is this?" Cat gave a jerk and a shudder and whispered, "Please help me, dear lady. My name is Prunella Peatmoss, daughter of Sophia and Samuel Peatmoss, sister of Bogley, who live down the road. You see, I was traveling by balloon to the hospital to have my tonsils removed, and while leaning over the rail to watch a flock of geese, I fell overboard and landed on your doorstep. The shock has caused me to lose my memory, and I was wondering if I might lie on your couch inside until I recovered." Cat began to moan and twitch and roll her eyes.

The old woman shook her head gravely. "My, my,

it *is* a shame that all you remember are the names of your family, where you live and where you are going. But don't worry. I'm sure a few moments out here in the fresh air will bring your memory back quickly. Perhaps I should call the hospital to let them know you're here. What hospital is it?"

Cat rolled over and moaned again. "I don't remember."

That night, the old woman left a dish of French Vanilla ice cream in the barn with a note: "For your tonsils."

The next day the old woman went to town to buy peppermint tea and arrowroot biscuits, and when she returned Cat was already on the porch. She was wearing a light blue robe embroidered with daisies, and on her head rested a wreath of golden maple leaves. The robe looked very much like an old kitchen curtain the woman had stored in the barn.

"Well," said the old woman, admiringly. "What have we here?"

"You mean *who* have we here," Cat smiled and tossed her head carefully, so the wreath would not fall over her eyes. "You are speaking to Graziella Grossinger, poetess. I live down the road."

"I didn't realize I had such interesting neighbors," said the old woman.

"You must have read my books, *The Wind in the Pussy Willows*? *Quivering Cattails*? No? No matter, I am too deep to be popular. But why am I here? What has snagged my sensitive heart? It is the way the sunlight shines through the colored windows, reflecting a rainbow upon the geraniums. Why, I could write a sonnet on it! Would you allow me to view it from the inside so I may absorb the beauty from all angles?"

Just then one of the old woman's cats leaped onto the windowsill. His eyes turned to slits, his ears lay flat against his head and his tail swished furiously, shaking a flurry of pink petals to the floor. He opened his mouth, showing sharp white teeth, and hissed at the stranger.

Cat picked up her skirt and left quickly, her wreath fluttering to the ground. "I must leave," she called over her shoulder as she ran down the road, "I feel a poem coming on."

The next morning, Cat was nowhere in sight, and the old woman sighed with relief. She went outside to rake up the falling leaves and put them on her rose bushes. As she scooped the leaves into a bag, she felt a tap on her shoulder. She stood up with a sigh, knowing who it was. Cat was standing at attention in a stiff white coverall with matching cap. On the pocket of the coverall was embroidered a mouse lying on its back, its legs jutting sharply into the air.

"How do you do, madam," Cat bowed deeply. "My name is Tootsie Wootsie Pfefferneusse, and I represent the Ketchum & Eatum Mouse Extermination Company. Now that fall is upon us, you are no doubt overrun with all manner of undesirable rodents. I am sure that a woman of your high standards doesn't want mice in her flour bin or fruitcake, so I have come to check your house and tell you just how bad it is.

"If things are as bad as I think — after all, it is a very old house — and all those dirty little creatures are right this moment scurrying about your attic, I will be most happy to take care of your problem. We guarantee satisfaction."

"Thank you, Miss Pfefferneusse, but that won't be necessary," the old woman said as she resumed raking. "I have five cats who take care of any mouse problem I might have."

"But are they reliable?" Cat asked anxiously. "Do they do the job? Perhaps they are old and sluggish, due to sitting around and eating too many sardines."

"Perhaps. But even so, what does it matter? I could learn to live with mice."

Cat looked shocked. "That's absolutely disgusting," she muttered. She shook her head and stalked off toward a little red van with the same mouse emblem painted on its side and drove off.

One week passed without any sign of Cat, and the old woman began to relax and hope that Cat had given up. Then one evening, a loud wailing and clanging startled the old woman from her reading. She looked out the window, and there was Cat, banging on a tambourine, swaying and twirling in a skirt made from twenty-five silk ties that the old woman had packed away in the barn to use in a quilt sometime. Gold-painted acorns hung from Cat's ears.

The old woman gasped. "Cat, you have outdone yourself!" Cat acknowledged the compliment with a modest nod of the head. "Ah, dear lady, it is your good fortune tonight to have before you Magda Pepperoni, gypsy fortune-teller who wanders the world...."

"You mean you don't live down the road?"

"Of course not. My tribe comes every year for the Pot Cheese Festival to sing while they squeeze the curd."

"I see," said the old woman, biting her lip, "and what can I do for you, Magda?"

"Ah, no, dear lady, it is rather what *I* can do for *you*. As I look into my crystal ball," Cat peered into a murky white marble in her paw, "I see a sad old woman sitting by the window in a large white house. And why is she sad? Because she is lonely and needs a new friend. And what else do I see? Aha, yes! I see a cat — an extraordinary cat — beautiful, intelligent, loyal — she jumps into the woman's lap, and the woman is happy once more. She cannot believe her good fortune...."

"That is incredible, Magda. You certainly can look into the future. For, you see, in a moment I shall return to my rocker and any one of my beautiful, intelligent cats will jump into my lap and I will be happy. Good night, Magda, happy trails!"

The old woman pulled down the shade and listened

to Cat banging her tambourine as she danced her way down the road.

And so it went all autumn, with Cat appearing day and night with a new plan to work her way inside the big white house. The old woman was growing weary of it. When would Cat realize she would never be anything more than a barn cat and give up?

Cat was growing weary too. Her imagination as well as her supply of costumes were giving out. She never thought the old woman would be so stubborn. The late-autumn cold that was settling in her bones was also settling in her mind and heart.

She decided to make one more attempt. She encountered the old woman digging up carrots before the garden froze. "Good afternoon, madam," Cat said in a prim, businesslike manner, "I am Marbelina Kumquat, and I am here to take the census. My job is to count the number of black-and-white cats in the village. I am told that you have five cats. Is this true? I will have to count them myself to verify the fact, so if you will kindly show me to your home…."

"That's it!" snapped the old woman. "I have had enough of this nonsense. If you don't stop bothering me immediately, there is going to be one less black-and-white cat in the village right now!" The woman grabbed her shovel and chased Cat out of the garden, across the road and into the woods.

After that, Cat came no more.

The old woman had no idea where Cat had gone. She knew that the food she put in the barn was disappearing, but she didn't know who was eating it. While she would admit this to no one, she actually missed the old pest and she was worried about her. She actually hoped Cat was warm and being fed, somewhere.

Cat had not gone away, just out of sight. When the first snow covered the bare trees, she climbed to the hayloft up near the eaves and came down only to eat. Sadness as well as the cold had now spread into her bones, for soon it would be Christmas. Christmas! She thought back to how it was when the kittens were around and remembered the good, brawling times they'd had. She wondered what they were doing now. Did they

ever think of her? They never wrote.

How wonderful, she thought, Christmas would be in the big white house! For so many years she had wandered down the road at this time of year, peering into the brightly-lit homes with their windows steamed from holiday cooking, their families laughing and decorating trees and hanging mistletoe. How she yearned to belong to such a home.

On Christmas Eve, the snow fell softly in the crisp, still air, and the stars shone bright enough to light the road for the old woman's walk to church. She sat in a back pew, snug and warm and content, and listened to the sweet, sleepy voices of the children singing about friendly beasts and angels on high.

She imagined how it must have been that first Christmas in the cold, smelly stable, with cow and sheep and cooing dove comforting the Child. The old woman closed her eyes and let her mind linger on the image. Then, without warning, there was Cat hovering near the blessed manger, dressed in shepherd's clothes, her eyes rolling heavenward.

The old woman whispered angrily, "Get out of my scene, Cat! You don't belong here. Have you no shame?"

Cat whispered back, "Why don't I belong? After all, I can sleep on the Child's feet and warm him. I can protect him from mice. I can dance for him and make him laugh. I can curl up under his chin and purr him to sleep. Why shouldn't I be there? At least *he* wouldn't turn me away."

Behind Cat's scornful twitch of whiskers, the old woman saw two small, fat tears ready to drop from Cat's bleary eyes.

She rose to join the congregation in the last hymn, "O Come, Let Us Adore Him," singing as loudly as she could, as if she could drown out the decision that was already rising in her heart, for she knew that Cat had finally won.

The old woman walked home slowly through the gently dancing snow, knowing that her life would be changed in a little while, and went directly to the barn. At first she couldn't find Cat, but then, by the light of the moon shining through the cupola, she saw her, a small huddled lump with a feedbag shawl around her shoulders and a dishrag scarf tied under her chin. She sat

on top of a basket of cabbages, sniffling.

"Cat?" the old woman called softly.

"Over here," mumbled Cat, quickly wiping her eyes. "Forgive me, but I wasn't expecting visitors." A twig of pine stuck out crookedly from a dirt-filled tunafish can laying beside the basket. Next to the can were four shriveled catnip leaves modestly tagged "To Cat, From Cat."

"What's wrong, Cat?" asked the old woman.

"My name is not Cat. It is Mrs. Rowena B. Halibut, and I am depressed because of cold and loneliness. My children have gone away, and I am alone in the world, and nobody cares." Cat sighed a long, quivery sigh, and another tear rolled down her cheek, over her mustache, onto her shawl.

"There, there, Mrs. Halibut," the old woman said softly, "I think I know just the thing to cheer you up. Why don't we go into the kitchen and share some eggnog?"

"Eggnog? Kitchen?" Cat was afraid she had not heard right.

"Yes, eggnog. In the kitchen!" The old woman knelt and scooped the old cat into her arms and tickled her behind her ears. "Merry Christmas, Cat!"

And so Cat joined the family in the big white house. The other cats greeted her with wary politeness — it was Christmas, after all — but no real affection. Cat didn't mind. She knew they would come around once she took charge of things.

On Christmas morning she sat inside the window she had chosen to be hers and basked in the sun. "I suppose," said the old woman, sipping her ginger tea, "now that you're respectable and live in a big white house, we shall have to give you a name."

"Don't worry," Cat smiled slowly, licking sardine oil off her paws, "I'll think of something."

There was just one week before the great feast of Christmas, and all the members of the attic mice family were throwing themselves into a flurry of busyness for the celebration. They had scrubbed and swept and polished silver and baked pastries and steamed puddings and wrapped secret presents and loved every minute of it. Omeletta flopped down after taking a tray of gingerbread cats out of the oven and sighed out loud, "I'm so happy, I just can't stand it!"

"You took the words right out of my mouth," said her mother, Gertrude, whose hands and face seemed always dusted with flour these days. Gertrude's mind was working as busily as her hands to think up a new way to show the mouse family's happiness, something beyond cleaning and feasting and trimming the tree. What they needed, she thought, was a tradition, a special Christmas tradition that would become a sweet memory as the years passed.

She and Arnold had such memories, lovingly brought out and shared with the children each Christmas. Arnold told how he and the other members of the Bachelors' Club at the University would go caroling, and then come back to the library for hot mugs of rum and imported cigars and good conversation. "Such a fellowship we had," he sighed, remembering.

Gertrude had been in charge of the churchmice choir before she met Arnold. How sweet it had been, she told the children, to lead the choir in their carols on Christmas Eve at the manger after Midnight Mass. The carolers had the Christ Child all to themselves as they sat on the splintery edges of the manger and sang their little mouse hearts out in the shadowy light of the church candles.

And, as a special gift, this year they would arrange a Living Tableau for the Child. Gertrude had a special talent for such presentations (the mice elders had once awarded her a plaque for *Unique Artistic Achievement*). She would choose an important moment in the Bible and would artfully portray it with the mouse choir as if it were a painting.

hen all was at the moment of perfection, she would whisper, "Freeze!" From that instant until she snapped her fingers releasing them, no whisker or tail would twitch, no nerve ripple or nose sneeze.

They would be frozen as statues. Oh, now and then a minor disaster occurred, such as in the homecoming scene of "The Prodigal Son." The little fellow who was the Fatted Calf was seized by a fit of giggling and fell off the spit. But the audience laughed in good humor, for he was a very young mouse and it was his first Tableau. Gertrude took five curtain calls that night and had to grant an encore, for which she was prepared ("Moses Parting the Red Sea").

"Ah, those were the days," sighed Gertrude. But she was not one to sigh and let it go at that. Someday this Christmas would be the old days to the children. Now was the time to start a tradition. Their own creche must be a good one, for what is Christmas without honoring the Child! Perhaps they might build one outdoors in the farmyard next to the silo. But how? Arnold was a literary mouse with no talent for carpentry, and Chester was the image of his father.

Could she and the girls do it? No, that would hurt Arnold and Chester's feelings. And, besides, the girls could do nothing together without fighting. She waited for inspiration.

On Sunday, as usual, they went on their expedition to discover the contents of boxes brought up during the

week. There was nothing of interest today except a box of old *Countryman* magazines, to which Amold would happily return when he was alone. He had noticed, in a quick skimming of the top one, an article on walking sticks that might prove interesting.

Then Omeletta, who had gone exploring on her own, squealed from a far corner under the eaves, "I found something! Wait a minute…I think…" She scratched and sniffed and coughed from the dust and finally yelled, "Hurrah! Guess what I found — I think it's a creche! Hurry, everyone, come see!"

The mice scrambled to the corner and joined Omeletta. They pulled and tugged at the box until they tipped it over and spilled its contents onto the floor. Not only was it indeed a creche, with thatched roof and an empty manger the size of a matchbox, it was also filled with toy animals of all description.

With great excitement the mice uncovered the objects wrapped in brittle newspaper blankets. "Look at this, Gertrude," said Amold. "The date on this paper is January 16, 1932! Why, this creche must have belonged to the grandmother of the house."

"Oh, look," whispered Prim as she held a blue glass bird up to catch the light of the afternoon sun. "And look at this." Omeletta laughed as she lifted a small, white wooden rabbit with a green waistcoat and drum.

"And this!" Chester shook a saltshaker in the shape of a turkey with holes in his tail.

"What a strange gathering," mused Amold. "One would expect to find the normal amount of cows and sheep, but these are quite unusual, I must say."

"There's more," said Chester, and he dove pell-mell into the newspapers at the bottom of the box. Up he came, as if surfacing from under waves, with several larger animals. With some grunting and heaving the others helped Chester bring the bulky creatures out of the box.

The mouse family lined the animals up against the door and examined them. There was a blue pottery pony from Mexico with a white flowing mane and poppies painted on his saddle. A yellow china pig. A fuzzy red reindeer with one gold antler. A black china pie-bird, his

beak lifted in song. Three monkeys joined together, their paws covering their respective eyes, ears and mouths. There was even a cream-colored calico cat, lying with her paws tucked beneath her.

Omeletta was all for leaving the cat in the box, but Gertrude, ever mindful of giving good example, would not allow it. "It is Christmas, children, and we must try to love everyone. Even a cat." At least we can try, she thought.

So they set about moving the creche to the barnyard. Prim got her red wagon and Chester the wheelbarrow, and slowly, with everyone steadying it, they wheeled the creche across the attic and into its spot by the silo. They were quite amazed at what they had done. When they sat down, Chester said matter-of-factly, "You know, there's no Baby Jesus. No Holy Family. No Wise Men, either."

The mice fell silent. "Whatever could have happened to them?" said Gertrude. "What good is a creche without the main characters?"

Arnold pulled on his pipe thoughtfully. His eyes met the eyes of his wife, who at that very moment had what she knew to be a divine inspiration. His eyes began to twinkle. Being a husband and wife in love, they often could read each other's minds.

"My dear," he said, "I think it's time for you to create one of your famous Living Tableaux. Think about it — what do we have here? Five mice — five exceptionally talented mice, I might add. Mice who never say no to a challenge — am I right?"

Gertrude, flushed and happy, agreed. "A marvelous suggestion! What do you say, children? Are you game? Of course, it's been so long since I've directed….

"Well, we're doing this for the Christ Child, and surely he won't be too critical. Now," she added, her mind already spinning with plans, "your father, of course, will be Joseph, and I will be Mary, and you three will be the Wise Men from the Orient. Aren't we lucky to have just the right number?"

"We have no Baby Jesus," said Prim.

"Hmmm," said Gertrude thoughtfully. "You're right. We need a Baby Jesus. Now, where shall we find him? What can we use?"

"How about my Baby Mousekins doll!" said Prim. "She's just the right size."

"No!" interrupted Omeletta vehemently. She thought that her sister's Baby Mousekins was the dumbest doll she'd ever seen, and ugly too. "I've got something better!" She looked around wildly, and her eyes fell on the wreath hanging on the farmhouse door. "The chestnut! He'd be perfect!"

They all agreed, even Prim, reluctantly, that yes, he would be perfect. And so they began rehearsing that very evening after supper.

For the rest of the week, the whole family pinned and clipped, scissored and sewed. They even made forays into the sewing room and kitchen downstairs for odds and ends of satin and cork and lace and crayon. They found a piece of green flannel with candy canes on it, just the right size to be a swaddling blanket for the Baby Jesus.

They rehearsed their carols in wonderful harmony. Amold sang bass; Chester, tenor; the girls, wavery

soprano; and Gertrude, a deep, mellow alto. In the evenings, when the dishes were done, they would gather in the living room and string panridgeberries for the tree, singing "It Came Upon a Midnight Clear." They wondered impatiently if that midnight clear would ever come.

Finally, it arrived. The moon shone full and bright, and a few snowflakes danced outside the attic window. The farmhouse sparkled with cleanliness and twinkling tree-lights, and the air hung with the fragrance of pine needles strewn on the floor of the creche. The toy animals circled the empty manger bedded with a thimbleful of straw. At the stroke of midnight from the grandfather clock downstairs, the solemn, reverent procession of mice began. As they ceremoniously walked toward the creche, they sang "We Three Kings of Orient Are." First came Joseph in a striped robe (cut from a kitchen towel), leading the way with a candy cane staff.

Gertrude followed, eyes lowered, her face framed in a blue satin mantle embroidered with pink stars. She

held the Baby Jesus chestnut tightly in her arms. Next came the Wise Men in order of age: Prim, in a blue lace robe (made from an old curtain) and silver thimble crown; Chester, trying not to tread on the hem of his purple silk robe (cut from a necktie) or to trip on the chain of paper clips hanging from his waist; Omeletta, in a tunic of gold sequins and fringes (part of a lady's evening bag), beating her tambourine and dancing in her bare feet to the music.

The Wise Men had begun to offer their gifts — three grains of barley, a patchwork pillow, a chocolate-covered raisin — when Gertrude's sensitive ears caught the sound of danger, a soft, padding sound. Terror fluttered her heart as she saw Max the cat coming slowly up the stairs — fat, mean Max, who was to be feared as much as the humans, even though his eyes were losing their sharpness.

What was he doing here? Had he planned to do them in on this sacred night? Gertrude could not know that Max, tired of the holiday noise and teasing of visitors,

had come to the attic to get away from it all and perhaps catch some sleep.

When he reached the top of the stairs, he collapsed in a furry, rumpled pile. Before he shut his rheumy eyes, he thought he saw two mice standing over a manger, two other mice offering gifts to a chestnut in the manger, and another, slightly wild mouse dancing and beating a tambourine. His eyes widened and his mouth opened and his tail grew thick and started to quiver.

At that moment Gertrude whispered the word "Freeze!" and the mice turned as lifeless as the toy animals. Joseph patted the Mexican pony. Mary cuddled the Child. Chester held out his gift of three grains of barley. Prim curtseyed. And Omeletta stretched her leg in an arabesque and raised the tambourine high above her head.

Not a whisker twitched, not a breath heaved their chests. The old cat blinked several times and began to drool, which embarrassed him. Mice in a creche! One

wearing a thimble, another shaking a tambourine! He decided his mind was wandering. He would go back downstairs, he decided, and find a safe, quiet place under a bed. He preferred noise to bewitchment. As softly as he had come up the stairs, he went back down, but at a faster pace.

The mice were jubilant! After all, to get the better of mighty Max was no mean feat. They hugged and kissed and wished each other Merry Christmas and sang "The Holly and the Ivy" all the way back to the farmhouse, where they sat down to the festive table spread with persimmon pudding and sugared almond cakes and freshly squeezed cider.

After the children, stuffed and sleepy, finally went to bed, Gertrude and Arnold sat together in the love seat and watched the tree lights blink.

"Tonight was truly a masterpiece, my dear," said Arnold.

"Oh, I'd say more of a small triumph," said Gertrude modestly.

"And the beginning of a tradition," added her husband.

"Yes, indeed," smiled Gertrude, her mind already busy with plans for the second annual production of *The Attic Players' Christmas Tableau.*

On a busy corner of a busy city street sat Babinski's Bakery. It had been there forever, or so it seemed to the old folks. They had gone there as children with their parents, when Mr. Babinski's grandparents had owned it and he hadn't even been born yet.

Then it had been a grand place, with sparkling white tile floors and "BABINSKI'S BAKERY — FAMOUS FOR ITS *BABKAS*" painted in flowing gold script across its main showcase window. It bustled with customers waited on by polite young clerks dressed in white coats and hairnets.

Now the floors were no longer shining white, most of the script had worn away, and only Mr. Babinski, old and stooped from years of bending down into ovens, waited on the customers. Most of them were faithful old-timers who depended on Mr. Babinski for their dark country breads and *chrusciki*, the little twists of fried dough dusted with powdered sugar, so flaky they fell apart as you ate them.

Neither the customers nor Mr. Babinski seemed to notice the gray weariness of everything. Every morning, before the first hint of light streaked the sky, he came down from his bedroom over the shop and set the breads and buns and doughnuts to rise. Then he pulled up the frayed green shades with their long crocheted pulls and swept the floor and the sidewalk in front of the shop, opening the door to let the sweet warm fragrance of yeast and vanilla and spice out into the neighborhood. These moments comforted Mr.

Babinski. He was filled with contentment. He was master of his universe.

But Mr. Babinski was growing concerned about his universe. He did not know how much longer he could keep the bakery open. Children who were once polite and respectful toward him had grown into rude and bold ruffians. Often they would lump together in front of the bakery and laugh at or frighten the customers. Sometimes, on a dare, one would run into the store and snatch a doughnut or a bag of cookies from an old lady and run off laughing.

At night it was even worse. Burglars had broken the lock on his door, cut off the cluster of bells that jangled when anyone entered, robbed the cash register and stolen whatever was left on the shelves, leaving a trail of trodden-on jelly doughnuts and creampuffs.

Mr. Babinski hadn't had a good night's sleep in weeks. He asked advice from the policeman who came in every day for a Kaiser roll. "Babinski," said the policeman, "you should get a dog. A big, old, mean, snarly, barking dog. That would scare those guys away. Robbers don't want to tangle with mean, old, snarly dogs."

Mr. Babinski said he would think about it. He wasn't crazy about getting a dog. His parents once had a dachshund that used to nip at his ankles and tear his pants. And he had had a cat that was almost as bad. She would hide behind the bakery door and leap on people. Once she pulled off Mrs. Popowska's wig when she bent down to pet the cat, and the old lady never came back. A dog might be worse. But he would think about it.

The next day he went for his usual walk to the soup kitchen with the day-old leftovers the robbers didn't take. On his way past Himmelfarb's Junkyard he noticed such a dog as the policeman had described. He was long, lean and black from the tips of his pointy ears to his curly tail, which seemed wrong for his body, as if it had been tacked on as a joke.

The dog was barking wildly as he paced back and forth in front of the pileup of rusting car frames and doorless refrigerators. Dented car doors, headlights, steering wheels and tire rims were scattered in all directions.

Mr. Babinski paused and thought that this dog certainly was master of his universe. He went to the sturdily chained gate and said, "Doggy, why are you barking?" The dog kept barking, but now Mr. Babinski

thought he heard a sad whine in it. He reached into his bag and threw a jelly doughnut over the fence.

The dog gobbled it up as soon as it landed, then licked the ground for any crumbs that might have escaped him. He stretched out his lean body — Mr. Babinski could count the ribs — and did not bark.

Each day after that, the baker threw a cinnamon bun or molasses cookie over the fence as he passed by. The dog began to wag his strange curly tail when he saw the baker approach. Mr. Babinski still did not put his hand through the bars to pat him, for Mr. Himmelfarb had said that the dog, Bruno, had such vicious jaws he could snap a man's hand off. Bruno, he said, was nothing but a low-down, good-for-nothing, mean, trashy mutt who needed a beating every day to teach him who was boss. He was so mean that even the animal shelter wouldn't take him.

And now that he was closing down the junkyard, Mr. Himmelfarb didn't know what to do with the dog. "Probably have to shoot him," he shook his head at the annoyance of it all.

Before his mind could stop his mouth, Mr. Babinski said, "I'll take him. I can use him to guard the bakery." Mr. Himmelfarb looked at the baker and said quickly, "You'd better take him now." He was afraid Mr. Babinski would change his mind if he thought about it.

So the baker, trembling with the enormity of what he had blurted out, grabbed hold of the chain. Bruno, exultant, freed from ugliness, let out a yelp of joy. His eyes glinted red in the sun, giving him a crazed look. Then the baker, his feet barely touching the ground, and the dog flew down the streets, crossing against the lights, never stopping until they reached the bakery. Mr. Babinski screamed "Stop!'" and the dog, surprisingly, did. Shaken from the mad race across town, Mr. Babinski was certain he had made a terrible mistake.

In a little while, however, he'd gotten Bruno calmed down and situated in a corner of the bakery by the radiator, one of his old winter coats laid out for a bed. In the kitchen, under the kneading table, he put two bowls. In one he emptied a package of frankfurters, which the dog ate greedily but neatly, one at a time. In the other, he put cornflakes and milk. The dog ate everything and, his nose ringed with milk, looked at Mr. Babinski with grateful eyes. The baker began patting the dog on the head, gingerly at first. Then, seeing the dog close his eyes with pleasure, he moved down around the ears.

"Now, Bruno," he said, "I know you'll do a good job protecting the store. But I don't want you to bite, just

scare. Bark as loud as you want, wake up the neighborhood, but don't hurt. Do you understand?" Bruno looked puzzled but wagged his tail. Mr. Babinski went to bed and fell asleep immediately — but not for long.

He woke and leapt out of bed, for Bruno was barking his wild junkyard bark, so high-pitched he almost squeaked. Then there was the sound of crashing and thrashing and yelling and cussing and finally heavy-booted feet running off. When Mr. Babinski got downstairs, he found Bruno quietly working his way across the floor, eating the evidence of smashed lemon pie.

The neighbors, who were awakened by the racket, and the police and Mr. Babinski all applauded Bruno for his excellent work. Bruno, who had not yet cast off his junkyard manners toward humans other than the baker, bared his teeth and growled low. After all, a guardian could not become too friendly. With one last menacing snarl, he went to his bed, curled up and slept soundly.

Word of Bruno's rout of the burglars swept the neighborhood as quickly as news of birth and death. All day long people came to praise and offer him congratulations and dog biscuits. But Bruno continued to bare his teeth and growl low and look away. Soon his admirers turned away also, and customers were beginning to be afraid again, this time of the guard dog who took his job too seriously. Despite their evening talks, during which Bruno licked the baker's face and brought him his slippers, the dog did not seem to understand that most people were good, and it was only the bad ones he should snarl at.

Soon it was Advent, and every day of the approaching Christmas was busy with preparation. The bakery was filled from morning to night with customers who wanted the delicacies of the season, the *babkas* and poppyseed rolls, the butterhorns and rye bread with dill, the honey cakes cut out in the shapes of the holy family and shepherds and angels. Behind the counter Mr. Babinski hung the red banner with gold and silver letters that his grandparents had hung at the bakery's first Christmas:

Wesolch Swiat Bozego Narodzenia!

"Merry Christmas to All!" it proclaimed.

From all of this happy bustling, Bruno was absent. He had been banished to the kitchen so he would not be underfoot, menacing the customers. On Christmas Eve, when Mr. Babinski finally closed the door and pulled down the shades, he let Bruno out of the kitchen and sat

down to talk with him. But the dog, still disgruntled by his imprisonment, looked past the baker, as if he were not there, and out the window.

**r.** Babinski sighed wearily. "Ah right, old fellow, I know you're angry with me. But you know it's your own fault, don't you? Never mind, it's over. We'll go to sleep and then tomorrow it is Christmas. We'll celebrate all day, right?" He patted Bruno on the head and went up to bed. The bakery lay still and dark and quiet. Outside, snow fell silently, capping street lights and parking meters. The moon shone through the many holes in the shades, turning the shelves and banner silvery. The dog was not sleeping well. His feelings were still hurt and he was quite hungry, for he had played the proud prisoner and would not eat the food the baker had left for him in the kitchen. He got up and walked around the bakery, sniffing at corners and footprints, hoping to find something to excite him.

He saw a few of the holy cookies left on a low shelf and his stomach growled and churned. He whimpered with anticipation and decided to eat them. Tomorrow they would be day-old and he would get them anyway.

With a quick nip, crunch, gulp and swallow, Bruno consumed the holy family, two angels and one shepherd with a lamb.

Feeling wonderfully full and drowsy, Bruno lay down on the old coat and slept. He dreamed of running gloriously free through snowy fields, with the two cookie angels flying above and slightly ahead of him. Then they turned into real angels with pulsating wings. The shepherd, with the lamb across his shoulder, was running with him too, crying, "Hurry, we don't want to miss this!"

They came to a barn with a glow the color of sunset coming from within. Inside, Mary and Jesus and Joseph smiled and welcomed him. Jesus held out his hand to be licked and Bruno obliged. It was the only hand he had ever licked besides the baker's. A comforting warmth spread through him, and he felt a melting, a cracking of hardness, a rushing surrender, as if anyone in the world could pat him, even Mr. Himmelfarb, and he wouldn't mind.

The scene began to change and shift; the barn and snowy field disappeared. The humans, still smiling, became cookies again.

He remembered nothing more until Mr. Babinski woke him with a gentle shake. "Merry Christmas,

Bruno," he whispered, and Bruno licked his hand and nose and ears as fast as he could. Then they sat down to enjoy a breakfast of *kielbasa* and hard-boiled eggs and *babka*.

Then some customers knocked on the door to wish the baker a happy Christmas. Bruno just sat there politely, wagging his tail and holding up his paw in greeting. And that was just the beginning. He didn't bark or snarl or curl his lip again. Ever again.

The baker was delighted, but while it was wonderful to witness the dog's changed behavior during the day, Mr. Babinski wondered what would happen when burglars came again in the night. Would Bruno open the door for them? He need not have worried, for the burglars, remembering the old Bruno, never came back.

One day, two friars came to the bakery begging for food for the poor. Bruno licked their sandaled feet and lay down on them to warm them. Mr. Babinski invited them to dinner, and they had a great time, eating, laughing, sharing stories. They had such a feeling of kinship that they didn't want to part.

"Why don't you come visit us?" asked the friars.

"We live just outside of town. You can take the bus." Mr. Babinski thought that would be exciting. A Sunday in the country! And so it was arranged that on the next Sunday, Mr. Babinski and Bruno would ride the bus to the friars' monastery. Bruno was on his best behavior and even offered his seat to an elderly lady.

At the monastery, they rang the bell at the gate, and an old friar with a sweet smile welcomed them in to meet all the others. When he saw the large, bright, cheery kitchen with many ovens, Mr. Babinski thought he had already gone to heaven. And Bruno rejoiced in all the new marvelous smells, inside and out, although he detected cat among them.

The baker and the dog were so happy that they did not want to leave. "Then join us," invited the friars. Mr. Babinski said he would think about it.

He thought about it on the bus ride home. How wonderful it would be to live in a place of peace, of fresh, clean air and trees and clear night skies lit by stars instead of neon signs. He could give the bakery to the soup kitchen, gather up a few cherished things — the babka pan, his mother's Christmas cookie-cutters, the banner — and just leave

for the monastery. Who would miss him? Yes, he thought, it was time to give up. The old life would be stored away in his attic memory, which he could visit again whenever he chose.

By the time they returned to the bakery, a light snow had begun to fall again. The street lights had just come on, and people were hurrying across the streets in leftover Christmas good humor. Three old ladies from the church were waiting for him at the door, laughing about the movie they had just seen at the Seniors $2 Matinee.

"Oh, Mr. Babinski," they greeted him, "we're so glad you're here. We need something — anything — for desert or our husbands will turn us out!" They laughed again at such nonsense, and as Mr. Babinski unlocked the door, they patted Bruno lovingly, calling him a schmoozer. Mr. Babinski filled three bags with apple tarts and prune-filled sweet buns and would take no payment. "Day-olds, leftovers," he said, "thank you for taking them off my hands."

They oohed and aahed and protested, as he knew they would, finally leaving with a trail of "God bless you!" and "What would we do without you!" behind them.

Homer, a tall, skinny teenager from the neighborhood, opened the door and poked his head in. "Hey, Mr. B., want your sidewalk shoveled? I'll do it for a doughnut?" Mr. Babinski smiled and nodded. Bruno went out to supervise.

The old baker watched them through the window. "How could I leave this place?" he wondered. "This is my home. This is where God put us to work out our lives. And I am wanted and appreciated most of the time. I have plenty to eat. I have warmth and good smells and the touch of a customer's warm hands in thanks. And I have Bruno. Why would I try to find something better?"

Homer left with a bag full of crullers and promises to return whenever it snowed. Mr. Babinski and Bruno stood quietly in the doorway. The baker's heart swelled with a quiet joy — was this the grace the friar had spoken about? — and a compassion for the stream of people on their way home from work, laughing, jostling, crossing the street. This compassion seemed to bathe them in the golden radiance of Bruno and the baker's Christmas miracle so that he could see only the goodness in their faces.

Mr. Babinski and Bruno leaned into each other contentedly, delighting in the universe that had been given them. And then they went in to supper.

A Christmas Tree for All Seasons

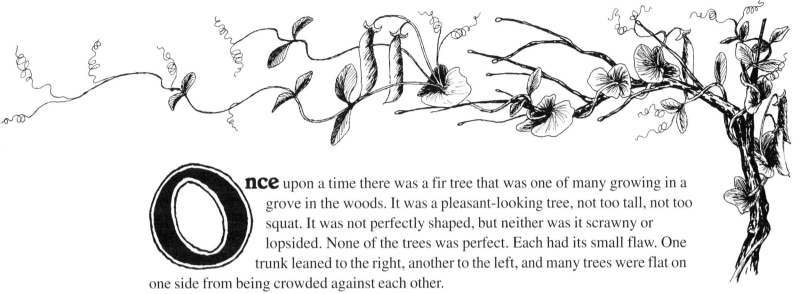

Once upon a time there was a fir tree that was one of many growing in a grove in the woods. It was a pleasant-looking tree, not too tall, not too squat. It was not perfectly shaped, but neither was it scrawny or lopsided. None of the trees was perfect. Each had its small flaw. One trunk leaned to the right, another to the left, and many trees were flat on one side from being crowded against each other.

But in December, all Christmas trees are beautiful, just as every newborn baby is the most marvelous of God's creations in his parent's eyes, no matter how he looks to others. With the dusting of fresh snow and the sweet smell of balsam teasing the eyes and nose, it was hard to find any tree you could call ugly.

A few days before Christmas, a little girl named Rose-Annette came to the woods with her father to find the most absolutely perfect tree. She searched and searched and went around in circles until she came back to where she had started. All the trees began to look alike.

She sighed when her father, with a bit of impatience, asked her which one she would chose. His toes were beginning to feel numb and his glove had a hole in the thumb and his sweater itched.

"I'll show you how to pick out the perfect tree," he said, "now just watch…." He put his hands over his eyes, turned around in a circle and stumbled over the snow 'til he touched the branches of a tree. Rose-Annette laughed, and then her eyes brightened.

"Papa, you're right! It is the most absolutely perfect tree!"

It was a very round, happy-looking tree that seemed to dance and bow in the wind over the excitement of being chosen. The very top of the tree curved downward, in the shape of a question mark without the dot, and the little girl knew that she would hang a very old ornament that belonged to her grandmother — an angel blowing a trumpet — from this natural hook.

Her father cut it down and trimmed the bottom branches off so it would fit into the holder. They carried it to the pickup truck and laid it gently on an old quilt. Then they drove up the winding hill, the road narrowed by snowdrifts, past the neighbors' houses already twinkling with Christmas lights on the doors and windows.

They set the tree up in the living room, and how proud it looked! "This is the moment in my life for which I was made," it thought. "I am beautiful. I am fulfilled. I give joy to everyone who looks upon me!" And how right the tree was! Grandparents and old friends smiled sweet-sad faraway smiles, as they remembered their Christmas trees and the heavenly smells of gingerbread men baking in the woodstove, with raisins for belly buttons and cinnamon drops for eyes. They remembered being bundled up in the sleigh for the drive to midnight Mass, the dark sky shot with stars, and their searching for *the* star.

And Rose-Annette's very young cousins and nieces and nephews and friends stood in awe and delight in front of the tree, their mouths frozen in *Ohs!* and *Ahs!* in the room lit by the candles and twinkling tree lights in the shape of icicles.

The tree was decorated with much love and little concern for fashion. Nothing matched. There was a glorious hodgepodge of ornaments — fragile, clunky, handmade — and each one had a memory. Some Grandma had left — a silver nutmeg, long-necked swans, hearts, bunches of grapes, angel and Santa faces, trumpets that really tooted when you blew them. Some Rose-Annette had made in school (her favorite was a wreath made out of a tunafish can). Some were gifts from friends — a stained glass star, a glass bell from Austria.

And then there were the cookies. Sugar cookie stars and trees and chickens and moons and gingerbread people and foxes and reindeer. Some were so heavy with frosting the tree tried hard not to groan with their weight. Rose-Annette hung them on the lowest

branches, the ones she could reach. Her mother would move them higher when the little girl was sleeping, but sometimes she'd forget. When she did, if you happened to wake in the quiet of the night, you would hear a stealthy munching and crunching as their dog, Moose, bit off the legs of gingerbread men and foxes and showed not the least bit of remorse.

Even though it seemed to Rose-Annette that it would never come, the great day finally arrived. The fir tree burst with pride and every part of him basked in the family's praise. "It is really the loveliest tree we've ever had," they told each other, just as they did the year before and the year before that.

Soon the holidays were over, too soon for the children, and they went back to school, eager to show off their gifts and talk about what they had done. Rose-Annette's mother looked at the tree, still handsome but drooping as its limbs grew more brittle, and said sadly, "Well, it's that time again. What a shame the Christmas tree can't last forever." She laughed to herself as she thought she sounded just like one of the children.

She unhooked each ornament and packed it carefully in tissue paper in the big box marked CHRISTMAS. Then she unwound the string of lights and put it in another box, but she left the tinsel and little bits of hardened cookies

dangling from the branches. She dragged the tree out the door and stood it up beside the house. When her husband came home, he would take it out to the garden.

That afternoon, however, the snow began to fall, first very softly, then heavily, in thick swirls. It whirled and blew about in gusts, and the school bus came early so the children would get home safely. By suppertime, a real storm had made a nest of snow about the house. They could barely see the comforting red lights of the snowplow blinking through the drifts outside.

The place where the Christmas tree had stood against the house became a huge white mound. The tree was completely hidden. It stayed that way for a long, long time, for this was the year of heavy snows and long freezes, and it was not until March that the tips of the fir tree's branches began to peek through the mound.

As the northwesterly gusts turned gentle under the April warmth, the tree, still with bits of tinsel dancing in the breeze, was now free to be moved. Rose-Annette's father carried it out back, and Rose-Annette tied to the tree's limbs pieces of suet that had been melted around bits of cracked corn and sunflower seeds. The

chickadees, nuthatches and phoebe birds flew around and nestled in the tree. Rose-Annette's mother said it reminded her of a line from a poem she knew from her childhood about a tree with robins nesting in her hair.

The weather grew warmer, and Rose-Annette jumped rope and played jacks outside. The birds left the Christmas tree and found more exciting food in and on the earth and new green weeds. A chipmunk ran up the tree trunk, stole the last piece of suet and knocked the tree to the ground.

This was a very special day, Good Friday, and it was the custom, her father said, to plant peas on this day, even if snow were on the ground. Her father hoed a row in the still-cold earth, and Rose-Annette planted the peas in a straight line, except for one spot when she sneezed. She found it hard to believe that by the 4th of July she could be eating fresh buttered peas for supper.

"Now," said her father, "we shall give them something to grow tall on." He went to the tree with his saw and cut off each branch as close to the trunk as possible. The needles, now stiff and brown, fell easily to the ground in little smooth piles, and Rose-Annette gathered them into the wheelbarrow. She took the needles to the strawberry bed and gently scooped little handfuls around each young plant. Later on, when she picked the

fat scarlet berries, she was certain she could taste the sweet fragrance of pine in them. She saved a sackful of needles, which she put away in her bedroom closet.

While she was doing this, her father stuck each lacy tree limb into the ground along the row of peas, their fingers entwined, like a row of dancers frozen in step. Soon the peas broke the earth and the vines began to cover the bare branches, making a green fence of curling leaves and tendrils.

One morning the little girl found the fence covered with small white blossoms, hundreds of them, as though some carefree hand had scattered them from the sky. And that night, as she sat on the steps on the back porch, she counted fireflies blinking on and off in the sky, in between the stars, in and out of treetops heavy with sleeping birds — one even came as close as the bottom of her skirt. But especially they twinkled in and about the pea vines. The Christmas tree, even in its different form, once again was hung with beauty and twinkled with excitement.

The blossoms turned to pods that grew fat and bubbly. Rose-Annette and her mother picked and shelled them, and, sure enough, by the 4th of July the family ate

fresh buttered peas. So too the other vegetables in the garden grew and were harvested in their season.

September came, then the first frost of October, and the garden rested. The only sound was that of the crisp wind rustling through the dried cornstalks and the chattering of birds chipping away at sunflower heads, searching for one lone overlooked seed. A jack-o-lantern, once frowning and fierce on Halloween night, sulked. His frown sagged down into his nose, and he looked like a sad, caved-in old building.

An artist came by and stopped to watch the few leaves left on the pea vines move stiffly in the wisp of cold air. He watched the sun draw shadow lines through the limbs and touch them with that special gold magic of early evening. He knew that he must catch the fleeting moment of beauty with his brushes. If he did, he would hang it on his wall to remind him always that there was beauty in every season of life.

November came in a gray sleet, and Rose-Annette began to dream of Christmas and the fun of making secret presents. She went to her closet and brought out her little sack of fir tree needles. There were just enough. She cut out enough muslin for three small pillows, sewed them together on three sides and then sat and thought about what she would paint on them.

She decided on three things that were dear to her: her black kitten, Nora, three daisies, and a gingerbread man. She got out her paints and finished the pictures in two nights. Then she stuffed them with the sweet-smelling pine, sewed up the edges and put them in her pajama drawer to wait for Christmas Eve. She could not wait to surprise her grandmother with the daisies and her friend who had moved far away with the gingerbread man. She saved the one with Nora for some special time when she might need to give a present. Until then, she would sleep with it herself and knew she would have happy dreams because of it.

On Christmas Eve her father burnt the trunk of the old Christmas tree, which he had sawed into three good-sized chunks, and it glowed a deep gold and blue. In this firelight their new tree gave back the glow, softly. It was the loveliest tree they ever had!

The artist sat in his room on Christmas Eve and listened to the bells of the city churches. He sipped his tea and looked again at the picture of the pea vines entwined on the fir tree limbs. "I think," he said, concentrating on one bright star out the window, "I shall call it *A Christmas Tree for All Seasons*."